THIS WALKER BOOK BELONGS TO:

_____

_____

_____

_____

To **THE WONDERFUL DELANEYS,**
with love from the silliest silly in the land.

First published 1999 by Walker Books Ltd
87 Vauxhall Walk, London SE11 5HJ

This edition published 2000

2 4 6 8 10 9 7 5 3 1

© 1999 Steven Kellogg

This book has been typeset in ITC Tempus Sans and Gararond.

Printed in Hong Kong

British Library Cataloguing in Publication Data
A catalogue record for this book is available from the British Library.

ISBN 0-7445-7828-0

THE THREE

SILLIES

Steven Kellogg

WALKER BOOKS
AND SUBSIDIARIES
LONDON · BOSTON · SYDNEY

Once upon a time

there was a farmer and his wife who had one daughter, and she was courted by a gentleman.

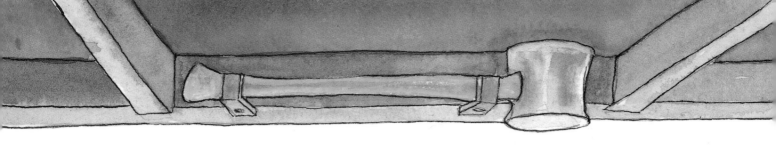

Every evening he stopped to supper, and the daughter was sent to the cellar to draw the cider.

One night, just as the daughter turned on the tap, she noticed a mallet in the beams, and she began a-thinking.

Suppose him and me was to be married.

And we was to have a teeny tiny son.

And he was to grow up to be a fine young man.

And suppose our son was to come down into the cellar to draw the cider.

And the mallet was to fall on his head.

What a dreadful thing it would be.

HERE LIES OUR SON, DONKED BY A MALLET

And she began a-crying.

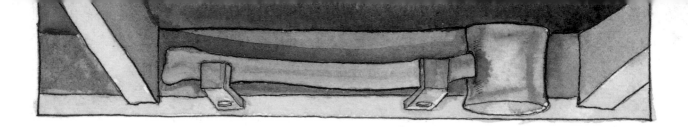

Well, the girl failed to return with the cider, and finally her mother went down to see what was a-keeping her.

"Look at that horrid mallet!" shrieked the daughter, and she confessed all that she had been a-thinking.

| Married. | A teeny tiny son. | All growed up. | Drawing the cider. | DONKED! | Dead. |

"Dear, dear!" said the mother, and she began a-crying too.

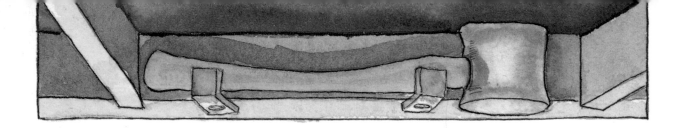

Then after a while the father went down to look for them.

"Look at that horrid mallet!" screamed the mother, and she told him all that their daughter had been a-thinking.

Married. A teeny tiny son. All growed up. Drawing the cider. DONKED! Dead.

DONKED

"Dear, dear, dear!" said the father, and he started a-crying.

At last the gentleman got tired of waiting, and he went
to draw a sip of cider for himself. And wasn't he surprised
to find the farmer and his wife and daughter a-sobbing and
a-screeching and a-swimming in the cellar full of cider.
   The gentleman burst out a-laughing.

"In all my travels I've never met three sillier sillies," said he.

"Now I shall set out travelling again, and when I can find three sillies who are even sillier than you three, I'll come back and marry your daughter."

And the gentleman left them all a-wailing worse than before!

After travelling a while the gentleman came upon an old woman who was teaching a cow to spring onto the roof of her cottage to eat the weeds that were a-growing there.

The old woman insisted.

Finally she got the cow up.

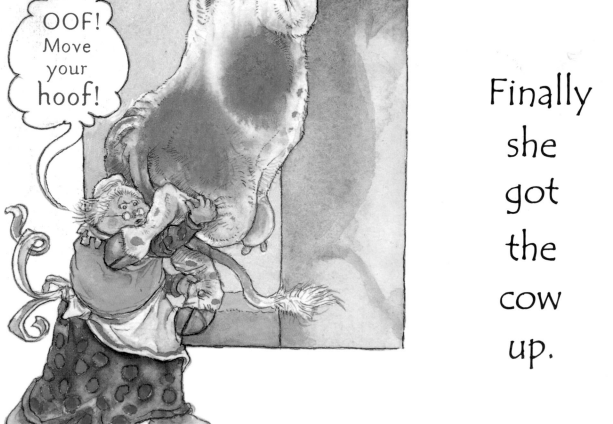

Then the old woman fastened a string around the cow's neck, and passed it down the chimney, and tied the other end to her wrist.

She'll be quite safe!
With this string tied to both of us,
she can't fall off the roof
without my knowing it!

WOOF!

"Quite daft!" said the gentleman, and he took his leave.

The gentleman hadn't gone far when he was overtaken
by a funeral procession, and he heard a dreadful tale.
It seemed the old woman's cow had tumbled off
the roof and the weight of the cow had pulled
the old woman into the chimney, and she
got stuck half-way up and was
smothered in soot.

A-TUMBLED

A-YANKED

A-SMOTHERED

Well, that was the FIRST big silly.

The gentleman travelled

on
and
on
and
on
and
on
and

on until he came to an inn at dusk. The inn was so full that the innkeeper put him in a double-bedded room.

Here's the room you'll have to share with Neddie and his teddy bear.

In the morning the gentleman was surprised to see his room-mate hang his trousers on the knobs of the chest of drawers and try to jump into them.

He tried over   and over   and over again.

But he couldn't manage it.

"Look, try it this way," said the gentleman, and he showed the fellow how to put his trousers on.

The fellow started a-pulling his trousers on and off and up and down until he had quite mastered the skill.

Then he burst joyfully into song!

Well, that was the SECOND big silly.

The gentleman's travels soon brought him to a village, and outside the village there was a pond, and around the pond was a crowd of people with rakes and brooms and pitchforks, a-whining, a-whimpering and a-wailing.

The gentleman asked what was the matter.
"Why," they said, "matter enough! The moon's
tumbled into the pond and we can't get her out."
The gentleman burst out laughing. "It's only the
moon's reflection!" he exclaimed. "Look up
in the sky. There's the moon."

Well, that was DOZENS of SILLIES!

But before the gentleman could complete his list, the crowd became a-restive, a-riled and a-riotous.

And so he took his leave.

The gentleman was heartened by the joyous welcome that awaited him.

"Dear, sweet, simple-minded sillies," he said. "In my travels I have met dozens of sillies who are far sillier than yourselves. Therefore I shall keep my promise. Let us be married at once!"

They hastened to the chapel.

After the wedding all of the guests
were invited to celebrate at the farmhouse.

The gentleman went to the cellar to draw jugs
of cider so that all could toast his new bride.

Just as he turned on the tap, the
galumphing footsteps of the dancers
above joggled the mallet loose.

Down it fell, directly DONKING the gentleman.

Then it bounced back and settled itself on the very beam from which it had been dislodged.

Stunned, the hapless gentleman keeled over and rolled under the flowing tap.

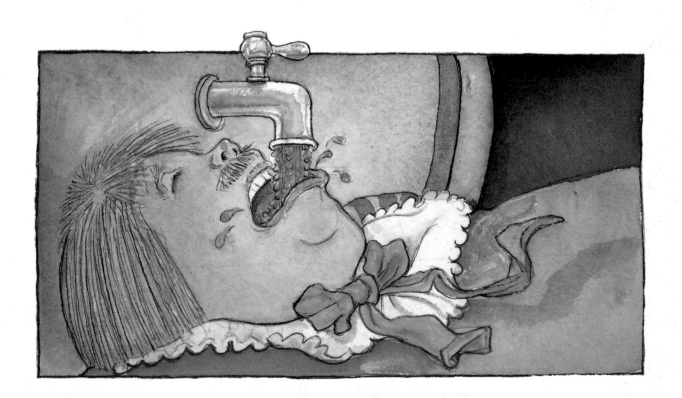

The entire keg of cider had drained into the
gentleman before he was discovered by his bride.
She a-hoisted him back to the celebration.

It wasn't long before the gentleman and his wife were blessed with a child.

The proud parents imagined a brilliant future for their son.

Finally the little fellow spoke for himself.

And so those three sillies set off around the world in search of silly adventures, and they lived for ever afterwards in blissful silliness.

The Three Sillies

STEVEN KELLOGG'S inspiration for this retelling was
'The Three Sillies' in Joseph Jacobs' 1890 classic,
English Fairy Tales. He says, "In Jacobs' notes and
references he gives credit to an earlier version of the
story from the journal *Folk-Lore* that 'was communicated
by Miss C. Burne'. He also mentions a version that was
'told in Essex at the beginning of the century', and
another from the collection of the Brothers Grimm."

Steven Kellogg's first book *Gwot! Horribly Funny
Hair-Ticklers* was published in 1967. Since then he
has illustrated over eighty picture books for children,
including several retellings of tall tales and folk tales.
In 1989 he was awarded the American Catholic Library
Association's Regina Medal for his services to children's
literature. *The Three Sillies* is his first book for Walker.
He lives in the USA.

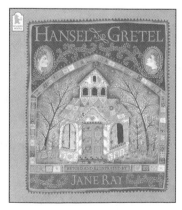

ISBN 0-7445-6960-5 (pb)

ISBN 0-7445-7810-8 (pb)

ISBN 0-7445-7825-6 (pb)

ISBN 0-7445-6956-7 (pb)